It never smelled fresh, and the air was all hazy; the people were wasteful... **and useless... and lazy!**

But then something happened
that none could explain.
It wasn't a bird
and it wasn't a plane.

Michael Recycle

written by
Ellie Bethel

Illustrated by
Alexandra Colombo

meadowside
CHILDREN'S BOOKS

There once was a town
that was really quite grimy,
where rubbish was left
to go rotten and slimy.

A green-caped crusader stupendously swooped, descending to Earth

with a great loop-the-loop!

He bounced off the Earth
with a thump and a bump,
and came to a stop
on a big rubbish dump.
"I'm Michael Recycle
for all that I'm worth!

I'm green
and I'm keen
**to save
planet
Earth!"**

"You must stop this now!

You've got to act soon.
There are towers of trash
that reach up to the moon!

Now pass on this message.
Get yourself heard:

Wasting is Rubbish.
Recycling's the word!"

Then crushing a can,
he gave them a wink...

...and vanished from sight
before they could blink!

with whispers of wonder
they turned to
each other,

and sister told Brother,

They recycled their paper,
their cans and their plastic,
transforming old junk
into something fantastic!

They even began a
"Be Greener campaign"
where they grew their own food
and collected the rain.

So proud was the town
of their green transformation
they threw a big party,

A Grand celebration!

They covered the town
using green toilet paper.
(But carefully rolled it
back up to use later!)

When Michael flew back in
to visit the town,
he didn't get angry,
dejected or down.

The people did everything
they had been told.
The streets were a
wonderful sight to behold!

"To Michael Recycle!
The green-caped crusader
our super-green hero,
our planet's new saviour!"

But Michael Recycle
was nowhere around,
he'd already gone on
to save the next town.

So if you should see
a dark green silhouette,
that streaks through the skies
like a super-fast jet,

just give him a wave
as you shout out
his name, it's...

...Michael
Recycle

For my very own little super-heroes,
Daniel, JJ & Ben.

E.B

For Mummy, Daddy (gnome), Pepi & Kay:
my super-heroes!

A.C

First published in 2008
by Meadowside children's Books
185 Fleet Street London EC4A 2HS
www.meadowsidebooks.com

Text © Ellie Bethel 2008
Illustrations © Alexandra Colombo 2008
The rights of Ellie Bethel and Alexandra
Colombo to be identified as the author
and illustrator of this work have been
asserted by them in accordance with the
copyright, Designs and Patents Act, 1988

A CIP catalogue record for this book
is available from the British Library
10 9 8 7 6 5 4
Printed in Indonesia